A man came to a hole.

A mole had made
the hole.
The hole was his home.

The man did not like
the hole.
"I can get rid of the
hole and the mole,"
said the man.

The man got his rake.
"I wish the mole had
not made this hole,"
said the man.

4

The rake got the mole up.
"I do not like this rake
in my home," said the
mole.

The rake did not get rid
of the mole.
The man got a lot of mud.

"I can pile the mud
on the hole," said
the man.

The mole did not like
mud in his hole, and
he did not like mud in
his home.

"This mud makes me
mad, but it will not
get rid of me," said
the mole.

The mud did not get
rid of the mole. So,
the man got a hose.

"I can get the mole wet.
Then I can get rid of him,"
said the man.

The mole did not like
to have a hose poke
its nose in his home.

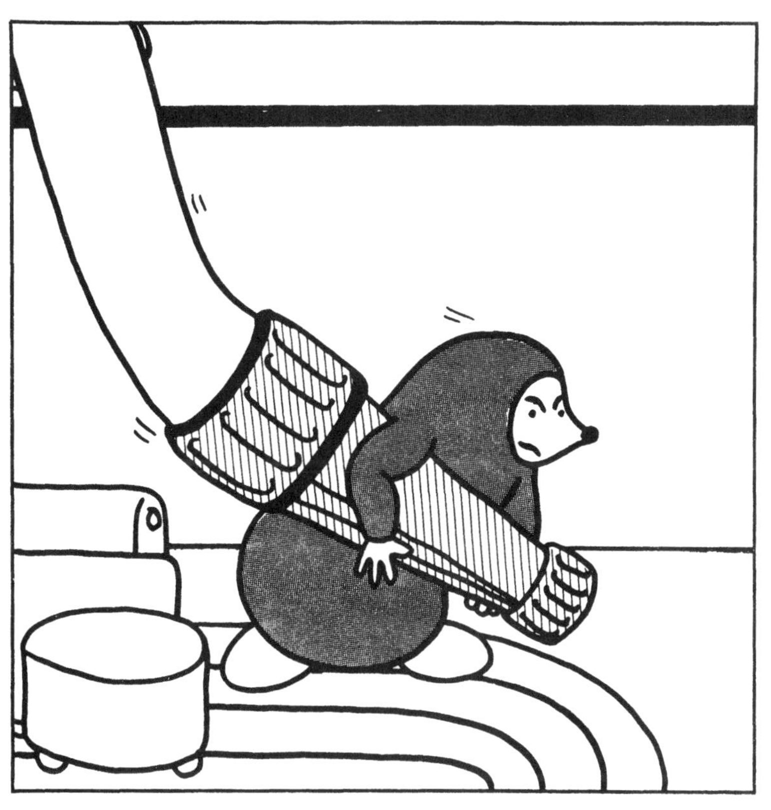

"But I can get rid of
that man," said the
mole.
"I can use his hose
to do it!"

The mole got the hose
and gave it a tug.
"The mole can not
take this hose," said
the man.

The mole put on the hose.
The hose got the man wet.

"I win," said the mole
as the man ran.
As the mole got up to
wave, the hose got
him wet!
Did the mole win?